Snowflake Hollow - Part 7

12 Days of Christmas, Volume 7

Lexy Timms

Published by Dark Shadow Publishing, 2021.

SNOWFLAKE HOLLOW - PART 7

First edition. December 1, 2021.

Written by Lexy Timms.

USA TODAY BESTSELLING AUTHOR

LEXY TIMMS

Copyright 2021 By LEXY TIMMS

Snowflake
HOLLOW
12 DAYS OF CHRISTMAS
PART SEVEN
USA TODAY BESTSELLING AUTHOR
LEXY TIMMS

All rights reserved.
Snow Flake Hollow
~ Part 7 ~
12 Days of Christmas Series
Copyright 2021 by Lexy Timms
Cover by: **Book Cover by Design**[1]

---

1. http://bookcoverbydesign.co.uk/

12 Days of Christmas Series

Find Lexy Timms:

LEXY TIMMS NEWSLETTER:
https://www.lexytimms.com/newsletter
Lexy Timms Facebook Page:
https://www.facebook.com/SavingForever
Lexy Timms Website:
http://www.lexytimms.com

Want to read more...
For **FREE?**
Sign up for Lexy Timms' newsletter
And she'll send you updates on new releases, ARC copies of books and
a whole lotta fun!
Sign up for news and updates!
https://www.lexytimms.com/newsletter

Snow Flake Hollow

SNOWFLAKES ARE KISSES from heaven...

She's not the biggest fan of Christmas – which is akin to a major sin in the little town of Snowflake Hollow. And with a name like Holly White, it's fitting that she owns the only B&B in town. The whole season is a huge deal, and the people coming to stay at the B&B are paying a premium to get the ultimate festive experience. She's trying to keep the guests busy, but Hank the Handyman just broke his leg trying to hang the lights. Now she has to figure out how to make the holiday festivities happen all by herself.

Enter Lawson Lane.

Mister green eyes, tall, dark and handsome, has come home to see his mother over the holidays, and is surprised to see Holly as the owner of the B&B. When he notices her struggling to get things done, he offers a helping hand. Seeing Holly again and enjoying the holidays might take a Christmas miracle—or he might end up with a lump of coal in his stocking.

It's 12 days of festive fun, what could possibly go wrong?

Lexy Timms brings you a Christmas holiday romance with 12 days of Christmas – each part of the story releasing like opening an advent calendar! Join in the holiday spirit with a festive read and some laughs to get you into the Christmas season.

Chapter Thirty-Seven

Holly

IT WAS STRANGE CLEANING up Mrs. Greene's room. She'd been staying at the bed-and-breakfast for so long, it felt like she was living there right alongside me. She was the first of the wave of holiday guests who came right after Thanksgiving, but now that Christmas was looming, she was moving on. I wasn't sure where. She'd never given me a direct answer. There were all those names on her card list, so it might have been one of them, but I wasn't sure why she would mail a holiday card to someone she was going to be staying with over said holiday.

Maybe it was one of her children she often talked about. They were far-flung throughout the country, apparently, so she could have been headed just about anywhere to see one of them. Mrs. Greene was one of those age-ambiguous people who was definitely older, but the exact degree of older could fall anywhere on a wide spectrum. I didn't know if we were talking her grown children were hosting their first holidays and she was going to surprise them with useful gifts like toasters and bedding they hadn't thought to get for themselves. Or if it was more along the lines of her grandchildren thought it would be fun to change up tradition and have their grandmother over for the holidays to spend time with their children.

Of course, there was also the possibility she wasn't going to spend time with family at all. She could have just been traveling around and ended up at the White Christmas Inn as part of her adventures but was now moving on. I could see that in her. She was a touch on the odd side and had a decided issue with personal space and kitchen safety, but she was unpredictable, and there seemed to be a touch of mischief in her. At least, I wanted there to be. I wanted to imagine her bouncing around the country, seeing different things, exploring towns, burning other people's bread.

Her leaving left a bit of a hole in the bed-and-breakfast, but it also left a mound of linens, a room to clean, and a new guest to prepare for. That worked out for me. It had been a few days since the festival, and I'd managed to steer clear of Lawson by keeping myself busy. Not that it had been all that difficult considering the amount of work it took to run an ostensibly holiday-themed bed-and-breakfast, in the freaking wannabe North Pole, at Christmas, with no help.

That was the kicker right there. It was all starting to really settle in for me now. I was aware of the ridiculousness of it all before, but now that I was wading through the peppermint-scented midst of it all, I was really having to face up to the situation I put myself in. Not only did I decide to chase my grandmother's dream for herself and start up the bed-and-breakfast, but I thought it would be a fantastic idea to do that during a major Independent Woman streak that deluded me into believing I could handle all the tasks of running the inn completely by myself.

I didn't need no man. Or apparently staff.

It meant managing reservations, dealing with the guests, cooking, cleaning, organizing, and evidently, being a damn elf fulfilling Christmas wishes.

I might have also been a bit more bitter right about that moment.

The truth was, I was still really hurt by how everything went down with Lawson. I didn't want to be. I scolded and chastised myself for it every time he made his way into my mind, which was far more often than I wanted to admit. In a way, it made it easier just to keep doing every-thing around the bed-and-breakfast I could possibly think of to do, including several things I just made up in order to give myself something to fill up the time that didn't involve going to his room and confronting him about the phone call.

There were no versions of that conversation in my head that actually turned out well, so I figured it would be best if I put as many barriers as I could think of between myself and doing that. And the thing was, I knew how silly I was being. I'd spent a good amount of time that first night and the next day talking myself through the whole situation and reminding myself there was nothing for me to be upset about. Not in the logical, sane part of my brain, anyway.

Lawson and I weren't anything to begin with, so I couldn't be upset that we weren't anything now. We never talked about having feelings for each other, or any kind of commitment, or even what we were going to do when it came time for Lawson to leave. We got wrapped up in the sparkle of the tinsel and the heady scent of pine trees and cookies, ended up kissing, and then tumbled into bed together.

That was it. Maybe it wasn't the sweetest story in the world when I broke it down that way, and the way things were rolling right along at this moment, we weren't going to end up as any kind of TV-special people cuddled up under themed blankets to watch. But I had to think of it that way. I had to dismantle the whole thing down into its basic elements and remind myself that was the way this all happened, and it was how it was going to end as well.

We never talked about any of this. We never mentioned it or questioned how things were developing. Lawson never told me there was a woman at home, but I also didn't ask. He didn't ask me about my relationship status or what might be going on in my social life either. I wouldn't have had anything to tell him even if he did, but that was beyond the point.

Now I was just trying not to let myself think about it. I just wanted to get through the rest of the season, have him and the other guests take their figgy pudding and leave, then focus on how I was going to attract more guests so I could make money at the inn during the off-season.

I finished cleaning Mrs. Greene's room and carried the linens and towels down to the living room. It was still early in the morning, but I wanted to make sure the room was ready even if the new guest showed up before the technical time for check-in. I'd encountered that issue already. A couple of times since the bed-and-breakfast opened, one guest would check out and another would appear at the front desk a couple of hours before check-in, wanting to get into their room, then be flustered and aggravated when it wasn't ready for them.

It was not a fun situation. I did get so annoyed at one of them that when they asked to speak to my manager, I walked out of the room, waited a few seconds, then walked back in and introduced myself as the manager of the inn. That gave me a couple of seconds of chuckling. But I'd rather avoid that happening. If the new people got there early, I was going to be ready for them.

Finished with that task, I headed into the kitchen to get everything ready for breakfast. I wasn't making anything elaborate. I didn't have it in me to try to put together a big spread. That morning, I was choosing just to be proud of myself for not plunking down a box of toaster pastries and instant coffee crystals and calling it a day.

I was lining a cookie sheet with slices of buttered bread sprinkled with shredded cheese to go with the bowl of fruit and boxes of cereal I intended to put out on the table when the kitchen door opened. I didn't need to look over my shoulder to see who it was. With Mrs. Greene gone, my options had dwindled down to one. I still looked. The last few days, I'd gotten breakfast done early and didn't linger around the kitchen to give him any opportunity to get to me.

That morning, he surprised me by slipping through the door earlier than he usually did. I didn't know if that was intentional, like he was trying to seek me out and knew this was the most likely place to find me unless he wanted to hang out around the washer and dryer for a meetup, or if he just felt perky that morning. Either way, he flashed me a smile and headed right for the coffee maker.

It was the routine we'd established almost immediately after he arrived, but it felt off now. The last couple of days, I'd gotten breakfast on the table early and didn't bother with coffee because the guests who drank the most of it had checked out. I left everything out and went about my morning, giving it some time to let everyone finish before going to clean up. When I went back, there were used coffee cups and a dirty carafe, so I could only assume Lawson had still gone into the kitchen and made some without me.

It also meant the guests wanted it, which was why I'd already brewed some while I got the food ready.

But Lawson was so accustomed to making a pot first thing and then keeping up with demand throughout breakfast, he didn't even notice the full pot sitting on the hot plate staying warm or the full carafe sitting beside it until he had gotten the beans out and was preparing to fill the reservoir. He paused and looked at the machine curiously, then glanced over at me.

"There's fresh coffee over here," he said.

"I know," I said.

"Why?"

"Because I made it. I was getting breakfast ready for the guests, and they are going to want coffee to start their day. So, I made coffee," I said matter-of-factly as I put the tray of bread into the oven and turned on the broiler.

"Yes, I understand the concept," Lawson said with a hint of a laugh. "I just meant why did you make it? You knew I was going to come down and make some."

I shrugged. "It's my job. So, I did it."

He laughed again. Something about him laughing aggravated me.

"You know, I haven't seen much of you in a few days. You've been getting breakfast on the table and disappearing before I've even had a chance to get up. I decided to get in here extra early today just to see if I could snag a look at you," he said.

I nearly melted. Which reminded me to check the cheese toast in the oven because anything having to do with a broiler was very touch and go in my kitchen. There was a very fine line between delightfully warm and bubby with just the perfect amount of melt and some toasty brown spots and everything getting burned all to hell. Besides, glancing into the oven to check the toast gave me the perfect excuse not to look at him. And hopefully to stop him from seeing the flush his words brought to my cheeks.

"I've had a lot to do," I explained. I stayed hovered over the oven, watching as the broiler melted down the cheese and the edges of the toast started crisping up. "I've been busy cleaning up after the guests and getting ready for new ones. I haven't exactly had a bunch of extra time."

The toast hit its perfect state, and I promptly took it out. Grabbing a spatula, I transitioned the slices over onto a platter, grabbed the full carafe, and walked out into the dining room without looking his way. I set the toast and coffee on the table and made myself smile at the guests. Vint reached out and snatched one of the slices, wincing and dropping it to his plate almost instantly.

"Careful," I said. "Those are just out of the oven."

He nodded and sucked on his fingers for a second, then leaned down and blew air onto the toast, dramatically puffing out his cheeks with each blow.

"It smells good," he said.

That made my smile feel more genuine. This little boy was really growing on me. When his family first checked in, I didn't think I was going to get used to having a child around all the time. I never spent a lot of time with children. There wasn't any opportunity to. I was an only child, born to an only child and a child with only one sibling who didn't end up having children. None of my friends had really young siblings. It wasn't that I vehemently disliked them or didn't want them around. I just wasn't used to them.

It worried me that I might not be able to be a good host for a child, especially one who was going to be around for such a long time. Maybe he would be one of those loud, obnoxious children who liked to run up and down stairs or jump off furniture. Or the kind who screamed and cried all the time, or asked a thousand questions, or tried to color on the walls.

And there had definitely been moments when he'd been loud. He'd screamed a couple of times. But for the most part, he'd been sweet, and watching him enjoy the Christmas craziness I'd been trying to put into place had made it all worth it.

Even on the days when I made the most involved breakfasts, I didn't like to hover around the dining room. It felt weird to stand there while the guests ate and talked. Usually that meant going back into the kitchen to make my own breakfast and eat before it was time to clean up. But that morning, I knew if I went back into the kitchen, Lawson would be there. I didn't want to have the conversation he tried to start up when he mentioned he hadn't seen me around much in the last few days, so instead, I headed upstairs to start the cleaning.

One of the ideas I was more proud of when it came to how I was running the bed-and-breakfast was little door hangers I left in each of the rooms. They resembled traditional do-not-disturb signs but instead had a list of requests or needs that guests could check off, as well as an area where they could write in anything else they might have on their minds. Having those made it possible for me to just swing by and get them from the doors in the mornings or evenings so I could quickly handle whatever needed to be done.

That morning there weren't any hangers, but as I walked by Lawson's room, I remembered what I said to him about cleaning up after the "other" guests. He hadn't let me clean his room, make his bed, or even put extra toiletries in his bathroom since he arrived. He brought the linens down to me, brought fresh ones up to his own room, and asked me where to find anything he needed.

That morning, I felt like I needed to give myself that distance. I went into his room and emptied the trash can, grabbed the dirty towels, and took a couple of dishes I found sitting on the corner of the dresser. I didn't know exactly why, but it felt therapeutic.

I brought the towels to the laundry room and brought the dishes with me into the dining room to check on the guests. They did not look happy.

"I thought it was getting better," one of them muttered.

"I've never experienced something like this at a bed-and-breakfast," an old woman who had checked in the day before said. Miss Nancy might have been old and liked to sit in the parlor in the afternoon, but she was certainly no Mrs. Greene.

"Can you even call this breakfast?" Vint's father asked. "Is this half a grilled cheese?"

This was a fantastic reminder of another reason I didn't like to hang out in the dining room while my guests were there.

I set my jaw, trying to keep control of myself. "It's cheese toast. My grandmother used to make it for me when I was a little girl. The bed-and-breakfast was her idea, so that is a dish in honor of her."

It was true that my grandmother used to make me the broiled cheese toast, but it wasn't until I started talking and heard the words come out of my mouth that I thought about having it in honor of her. They didn't need to know that. The toast was delicious, and they should have just been enjoying it rather than seeing festive flaws in its existence. Or mine.

Chapter Thirty-Eight

Lawson

SOMETHING WAS DEFINITELY up, but I was damned if I could figure out exactly what it was.

Holly and I had been having a great time, I thought. We were even bordering, if not having tumbled right on over, into relationship territory after we slept together. Going to the festival was supposed to be a solidification of that, and indeed, it felt like it was for the first part of the time we were there. I even got to look like the coolest dude ever with the clown dunk and then dipped her for a kiss.

Then, out of nowhere that evening, she just decided she wanted to go home, and I had barely seen or heard from her since. And when I had, she was cold and distant, like something I said bothered her or I had done something to upset her. I knew enough about women to know that asking what I did was tantamount to doing it all over again, so I dedicated quite a bit of mental space to going over the last few days and figuring out what in the world I possibly could have done to make her so angry and upset.

Days later and I still had nothing.

She had barely spoken to me on the way back to the bed-and-breakfast, so I was pretty sure it wasn't something I'd said then. She also didn't kiss me good night, and though I waited up for her, she didn't come back into my room after finishing up downstairs either. I had hoped for another night of being curled up with her, but apparently, that wasn't in the cards.

The next morning, I woke up to silence and realized I hadn't even changed out of my clothes, hoping she would join me for the night and I could get undressed then. It was presumptive, sure, but I liked the idea of not getting comfortable until I knew for sure she wasn't going to make it, and then I just dozed off in the bed with cooking shows on TV.

Over the next few days, she was elusive. It was like trying to catch a wet dog; she avoided me or slipped out of rooms right as I got in them. I couldn't seem to get a bead on her, and she was usually gone well before I got into rooms she had been in. I tried not to think something was wrong and that she was just busy, but it was hard not to think it. It was almost as if there was a glaring sign in her absence that said whatever we had was gone or at least was on pause.

Breakfast was just sad. I tried to find her by getting up early and meeting her down there, but she had already come and left, leaving behind a phoned-in breakfast of bland breakfast cereals, apples, and toast or a basic pastry. There hadn't been any coffee on those days, and I didn't know if she had just not made it because she didn't feel like it or if it was meant to be some sort of message.

I'd been making the coffee and occasionally surprising the guests with the coffee toppings bar since I got to the bed-and-breakfast. It had become part of my daily routine, and Holly knew that. Maybe by not making the coffee on the mornings when she got breakfast finished so early, she was trying to subtly express to me that there was a place for me and I needed to fill it.

Or that she had accepted that was my responsibility and she wanted me to keep up with it, even when she wasn't there to see me do it.

Or that she was acknowledging my role in her life and projecting to me that she felt the same way.

Or maybe I was just reading far too far into her not making coffee early when she knew the guests would have no problem whatsoever speaking their minds and letting her know if they were missing their usual cup.

So I made the coffee like I always did, and Holly disappeared into various parts of the house or her office.

Holly was apparently locked in her office most of the time, and when she wasn't, she was somewhere on the grounds doing some task. More than once, I went out looking for her, finding myself having just missed her putting up a ribbon on a window or taking out the trash to the curb. If I didn't know any better, I would think she was keeping an eye out for me specifically and anytime she saw me was diving behind a hedge or something.

Sometimes I would get downstairs, look for her, and realize her car was gone. Hours later, it would have returned, but there was no sign of her, and guests would mention that she had come by their room to ask if they needed anything and then disappeared. Whatever she was doing, she was getting her steps in for sure.

Another morning and another sad breakfast seemed doomed to be my reality when I headed down the stairs toward the kitchen that morning. I was half-tempted to go into my own pocket and order something for delivery for the guests and myself, but I had hope that maybe something would be different. The distinct lack of smells coming from the kitchen was enough to tell me that was not the day.

But there was one very specific change. When I walked into the kitchen, the coffee was already there. Along with an extra carafe. Maybe this was the message.

The table had fourteen chairs, but there weren't that many guests there. Vint and his family sat where they usually did in the center of the table, while the newer guests were mostly gathered together on one end, and I got the impression they were together in some way. An elderly lady sat at the head of the table, likely the matriarch of the crew, eating what looked like toast with shredded cheese melted onto it with an expression somewhere between age-wise calm and hot, seething, religious rage. The kind of rage most people only work up when they talk about their enemies from high school.

High school enemies would be familiar to the girl at the farthest edge of the gathered group. She couldn't be more than fourteen, with the trappings of youth and sullenness that generally come from the onset of acne, too many hormones, and not enough experience to know that every inconvenience isn't the end of the universe. She looked down at the plate in front of her and sighed in the way that only teenagers can manage and rolled her eyes so hard I thought she might have had a stroke.

"I thought everything in this place was going to be festive," she whined, not even bothering to take out the wireless earbud in both ears or her eyes from the phone that was likely one step from being surgically grafted to her palm. "We don't even have any eggnog."

It was at that moment that I noticed Holly was in the room. She was standing at the other end of the table with a carafe of coffee in one hand and a plate with a stack of unbuttered toast in the other. She was wearing an expression I could only compare to that of a lion in front of an injured zebra. Whatever was about to come out of her mouth would be eviscerating, mean, and most likely filled with four-letter words that tended to catch FCC fines on television.

She was about to snap. I could see it in her eyes. She was roughly a second or two away from throwing the coffee and morphing into a real-life grinch right before our eyes. I wondered if the sudden lapse in Christmas boot camp training was the reason she had become unhinged. She was left out in the cold with the expectations of Christmas-goers and no direction to help them in.

Then it hit me that I made that whole thing up. It really wasn't all that intense, after all. Not nearly as intense as the fistfight Holly was about to start with a girl who still had some baby teeth left.

"This way," I said softly as I came up beside Holly and took one elbow, leading her away and back to the kitchen.

She didn't hesitate or pull away from me, not at least until we were through the archway to the kitchen and she was out from the watchful eye of the old woman at the head of the table. Thankfully, she seemed to resist the temptation to slam the carafe down and instead shoved it onto the heater. The plate of toast wasn't as lucky. It was tossed onto the kitchen counter, and bread went everywhere.

Holly threw herself into a chair and sat, staring into the center of the kitchen table, eyes wide, but not saying anything. I looked back from her to the table, where the guests were starting to whisper amongst themselves. Then I looked back to Holly and took a breath.

"You stay here and cool off for a sec, okay?" I asked. I didn't wait for a response before I was through the arch and back out in front of the breakfast guests and their sudden silence upon my return. "So, Holly wanted to keep this a secret, but the reason there isn't eggnog now is because we are going to have some later."

"Later?" the girl asked, apparently able to hear me over whatever was playing on her phone.

"Yes, and it won't be the old store-bought stuff that's all thick and sweet," I said.

"I hate that stuff," the old woman said. "Back in my day, eggnog was proper. And had whiskey in."

I cleared my throat and nodded.

"Right, well, no promises on alcohol, but we are going to make some that will be waiting for you this evening. I promise, it will be good. We will have it available in the living room for an old-fashioned singalong around the campfire."

I saw the slight veil of approval cross the old woman's face, followed by a prim smile. Even the teenager looked happy about it, though I was sure she would be thoroughly embarrassed and tweet about the experience as if she were encountering alien life forms later. Still, a patch over the disappointment.

As I was speaking, I caught sight of Holly, back in the doorway, and I could just feel the thousand lethal icicles her eyes were digging into my back at that moment. I didn't need to turn around to see them. I could feel their heat as if Superman were burning a hole in my back with his laser vision.

"Well, that sounds just fine," the old woman said, nodding. "Reminds me of old Leroy, God bless his soul."

"Was that your husband?" I asked, desperate to find something to talk about that didn't involve turning around and seeing Holly.

"Indeed, he was," the old woman said. "Gone these thirty-five years next March."

"Oh, wow, he must have been very young. I am so sorry," I said.

The old woman waved the comment away and scratched behind her ear. When she did, I noticed the giant diamond earring being complimented by the even larger diamond on her finger.

"No, he wasn't," she said. "He was a cantankerous and frugal old man. He just wasn't one for very long when I married him."

"Oh," I said.

"Did that old woman murder her husband?" I asked quietly as I picked up one of the empty plates.

The guests had finished their breakfast and retired to do whatever it was they planned on doing for the morning. The old woman—Nancy, I learned—had simply gone back to bed. Part of her daily routine was to get up, get breakfast, and then nap for an hour before continuing her day.

"I don't know," Holly said briskly, stacking a plate on top of another and swinging them off the table to head back to the kitchen.

"I just would like to know if I was sleeping under the same roof as a character from *Arsenic and Old Lace*," I said.

There was no response from the kitchen.

Chapter Thirty-Nine

Holly

APPARENTLY, I NEEDED to whip up a brochure for the bed-and-breakfast. And it wasn't going to take a lot of effort to fill it in since Lawson kept insisting on adding things to the schedule. Of course, he didn't think it was important to throw me a little heads-up before announcing them, so that might make it a bit more challenging to keep the guests in the know.

I turned the faucet on with a harder push than I really needed to and went to work washing the dishes. Lawson came into the kitchen behind me, and when he appeared at my side, he had a huge grin on his face.

"I guess our Christmas activity of the day has been decided for us," he said.

It probably shouldn't have surprised me that he sounded delighted by the whole concept. Not just to have another Christmas mission to do, but that it was a surprise, and now we had to run around trying to figure it out. I sincerely wondered if he had a soundtrack of seasonal music going on in the back of his mind while all this was going on. Maybe a commercial break or two of this was a made-for-TV movie he had managed to fling us into without my realizing it.

"Actually, you decided it," I said. "They just pointed out we didn't have eggnog. You're the one who decided it was a good idea to tell them we would make it for them."

He shrugged. "I guess that's true. But it sounds like fun, doesn't it? And you have to admit they'll feel really special having homemade eggnog. I doubt any of them have ever had it."

"I don't know how you possibly think we are going to pull off making eggnog. I don't even know what's in eggnog."

"I don't know all the ingredients either. But we can find a recipe. And it can't be all that hard. We just work on it until it tastes right," Lawson said.

"Well, that won't be helpful for me since I don't know what it tastes like. I've never tasted it," I said.

He gasped and looked at me with a mock horrified expression, pressing his hand to the middle of his chest like an old woman who just watched a hip-hop music video for the first time.

"How is that possible? Not that you're going to be auditioning for the ghost of Christmas past anytime soon, but you are definitely an adult. How did you get to this age without tasting eggnog?" he asked.

"It has just never interested me. It's all thick and slimy-looking and kind of weirdly yellow. Gran was never a big eggnog drinker, so I just never tried it. And for your information, I have also gotten to this age without ever getting a picture sitting on Santa's lap or eating a Christmas goose."

"You've never sat on Santa's lap?"

"No. Apparently my parents brought me when I was a baby, but I started crying, so my mother held me for the picture. Then after that, I cried every time we got in line, so they decided it just wasn't important enough to put me through that. Then my grandmother figured the same thing. A child freaking out sitting on the lap of a stranger in a costume doesn't exactly say happy holidays," I said.

"Alright, I'll give you that. The whole Santa's lap picture might not be right for everyone. And I've never eaten goose either. But eggnog is... eggnog. It's just part of the Christmas season. Everyone has had it," he said.

I shook my head and put the dish in my hands in the drainer along with the others from breakfast. "Not me. And even if I had tasted it before, it would have come from a carton from the store."

The hurt inside me was getting stronger standing there so close to him, talking like there was nothing going on. I moved around him to put the food back in the refrigerator and start cleaning the counters. I decided to do a little test. These last few days, I'd been going back and forth with myself about whether I should have tried to talk to Lawson about what was going on and try to sort out our feelings. I wanted to know how that would go.

Spritzing the counter with cleaner, I started wiping it down. Without looking at him, I tried to toss out as casual a question as possible.

"So, do you have any plans you're looking forward to for when you go home?" I asked.

I was trying to get him to admit he was leaving soon, and maybe even that he was seeing someone back there. If he just came out and said those things to me, at least I would know he was being up-front and honest with me. It would feel less like I was being used or that I was just some kind of vacation fling he hadn't put any real thought into if he was willing to lay it all out there.

"I hadn't even thought about it," he said.

That stung. At least he could have been straight up with me. I didn't need him to get into any details or gush about Monica. I didn't even really want to hear her name come out of his mouth again. But I did want to feel like he at least had enough respect and care for me that he wouldn't try to be shady about it. Him skirting around the whole topic just made me feel like everything that happened between us, all the special moments and the feelings I thought were there, hadn't been real at all.

I was upset, and the hurt was even deeper now, but I wasn't going to show it. I didn't want to be that girl. The last time I let myself get that worked up over a guy and let him manipulate me because he could tell how emotional I was over him was high school, and I wasn't going to do that again. I also wasn't going to be the girl who took things too far and put too much emphasis on something that wasn't even there.

Showing it would just cause drama, and that was definitely not something I wanted to do while he was still a guest. It wouldn't do anyone any good. Once he was gone and the season was over, the glitter and wrapping paper fumes would leave my brain, and I'd be able to think clearly again. I'd get over him, and it wouldn't seem like such a big deal anymore. At least, that was what I was going to tell myself on repeat until I believed it.

Besides, Lawson was the one who'd promised the other guests homemade eggnog to make their holiday season all it should be. Now I had to deliver, but there was no way I was going to do that all by myself. If he wanted to get all pioneer time on this thing, he was going to have to help me figure it out.

"I'll be in my office. You look up recipes and make a list of what we'll need. I'll see you later to go to the store," I said.

Before he could respond, I walked out of the kitchen and went first to the laundry room to get a load going, then went to my office. I shut the door behind me and sat down at the desk, dropping my head forward with a groan. This was ridiculous. Why was I feeling like this about him?

I only allowed myself a few seconds of moping before I sat up and went to work. I needed to really start making plans for what was to become of the bed-and-breakfast during the non-Christmas season. I wasn't going to be able to rely on the income from just the November and December months to see me through the entire year, especially not this first year. That meant I needed to be able to draw attention and get guests there even in the middle of the summer.

Part of me had briefly considered staying Christmas-themed all the time. It would give guests who were aching for that seasonal spirit a bit of a reprieve during the long stretch of non-Christmas season during the year and build up more excitement that might lure guests back for the actual holidays. It sounded like a good idea at the time, but then I reminded myself that would mean continuously keeping up with the holiday decorations and activities.

I just didn't know if I had that in me. I might not have that in me even if I was a Christmas person. Even the most hard-core of the seasonal devotees around Snowflake Hollow put up patriotic buntings, dragged out their grills, and lazed away the hot summer months in inflatable pools and yard sprinklers.

So, I needed something else. Something that would make people want to come here no matter the time of year and would keep them coming back or telling their friends and family so they would want to visit. That was my mission.

I'd managed to make a few notes and jot down a couple of vague ideas when I heard a knock on my office door and looked up to see Lawson poke his head inside.

"Hey," he said.

"Hi," I said. "Did you find the recipe?"

"I did. But I realized there was something else we needed to work on. We could probably do it while we are out, too, but you could start getting your brain working."

"Okay. What do we need to do?"

"Make a list of songs for the singalong," he said. "Meet you on the porch in a few."

He walked out of the office, and I let out a sigh. We were having a damn singalong.

Chapter Forty

Lawson

"SHOULDN'T WE JUST TAKE one car?" I asked as we got into the driveway.

Holly had walked ahead of me outside and was fishing in her pockets for her keys, heading toward her car, and froze. Slowly, she turned on her heel and sighed, stuffing her keys back in her pocket and heading toward me again.

"I suppose," she said, passing me and opening the car door for herself.

I stood at the back of the car and shrugged. Sure, she was apparently distant enough to not want me to open the car door for her, and to assume she was going in her own car until I pointed it out, but at least she was willing to ride with me. So that was something.

I climbed in the car and hit the ignition button, firing up the engine and cranking the heat up. Holly pulled her arms over her chest and shuddered. There may not be snow, but it sure was wintery in Snowflake Hollow, weatherwise.

"The heat will kick in in a minute," I said. "Probably just in time for us to get to the store."

I didn't know if I actually expected a laugh, but if I had, I would have been disappointed. It wasn't stony silence, per se, but it was silence, nonetheless. Shrugging, I put the car in gear and backed out of my spot, deftly missing the mailbox by a few inches and causing her to roll her eyes.

The drive over was quiet, and I was thankful my car connected to my phone and started streaming music immediately. I was also thankful that the last station I was listening to wasn't Christmas music. I had the sneaking suspicion Holly might rip the radio out of the car and send it over the Newton Bridge if it was.

Instead, David Bowie came through the speakers, and I even caught a brief glimpse of Holly's leg bouncing a bit as he crooned. The car warmed up considerably by the time we reached the bridge that crossed over Newton Creek and into the suburban area around the heart of town. It was where the larger stores were, and while there were no big-box places in town, there were a few catch-all shops that had a little bit of everything that weren't terrifying mazes of guesswork.

Bob's General was just over the bridge, and I pulled in there, parking near the door. It had been there longer than Mary and Brighton's up on Main Street and tended to be on the calmer side. They were pretty dead this time of day, but they were one of the few stores in town that I knew would carry all the ingredients we needed for the eggnog if we didn't want to brave the grocery store. A lot of places might have the carton stuff in a cooler by the front door this time of year—probably all of them, honestly. But unless we wanted to go into the holiday grocery store crowds, this was where we were going to find everything that went into the eggnog itself.

Including the rum.

Bob's General had all the ingredients and none of the overexcited crowds. Or, rather, Bob's General had all the basic ingredients, and the tiny back store that was technically not really there, but totally was if you talked to Bob about it, had the booze. I had grown up with the knowledge that Bob got away with this bit of illegal rum-running by simply supplying the local cops every year for their holiday parties free of charge. That and a healthy discount kept them from busting him.

Little did they know he never put prices on anything back there because he would mark up the sale price enough to make the discount not mean anything when they checked out. Bob was a shrewd old man, whose daddy used to have to outrun the law in a modified early stock car. He often liked to tell the tale of how his uncle had helped start a whole town just south of Snowflake Hollow just based on running liquor past the cops.

"Howdy," Bob said as we walked in the door. "Oh, hey, Lawson. Who have you got here?"

"Hey, Bob," I said. "This is Holly. She owns the mansion on the hill that's a bed-and-breakfast now. She used to live around these parts."

"Matilda White was my grandmother," Holly said. "I used to come in here with her when I was younger."

"No kidding," Bob said. "I remember Matilda. Good woman. It was sad to hear she was gone. I tried to find out about a wake or a viewing so I could go pay some final respects, but I couldn't find anything."

"She didn't want any of that," Holly said. "She always said she would rather people have memories of her alive rather than of her lying in a coffin."

"Well, then there you go. Glad she got what she wanted. You say you own that mansion now?"

Holly nodded. "That was also what my grandmother wanted."

"Good for you. I always wondered what was going to happen to that old place. Nice to meet you, Holly."

"Nice to meet you," Holly said in a tone that was markedly different than any she had used with me in a few days.

"What are you folks looking for?" he asked, then seemed to have an idea. "Oh," he said and then did a gesture beckoning me to come closer. "If you're looking for some last-minute gift ideas for the young lady, I have a rack right over here that you could peruse," he whispered.

I looked in the direction he was gesturing gently toward and saw a small wooden four-way that looked like it had been there as long as the store had been open. On it, he had a selection of trinkets and cheap jewelry, along with a rather eye-opening collection of lingerie. Along the top of the display was a sign that read, "Christmas Lover's Collection."

"Thanks, Bob," I said to a grin and a wink from the old man.

Holly had grabbed a small hand cart and was already halfway down an aisle when I joined her.

"So," she said, "what exactly are we here to get?"

"Ingredients for eggnog," I said.

"Which are?" she asked, rolling her eyes.

"Well, I would think you should start with eggs."

Holly stopped cold in her tracks in the middle of the aisle.

"Please tell me you know what goes in eggnog. Please tell me that," she said.

"Maybe," I said.

"Ugh," she grumbled and stomped away to the refrigerated section, where the egg cartons were sitting. "Eggs, what else?"

I tried not to let it show, but I knew my shoulders sagged a little. Holly and I had so much fun, and now she was standing here reacting like I was her annoying teenage brother, causing her havoc for the sake of my own amusement rather than what we were. Whatever we were. Something that felt a lot like lovers.

Maybe she was just over it?

"Whipping cream," I said, trying not to sigh. "Milk too, but you should have some of that."

"No, actually," she said, almost disinterested. "Ran out of that this morning."

"Ah, well, good," I said. "I mean, good that we are here shopping, not that you ran out." Her eyes rose to me for a moment, and I shifted from one foot to the other. "Actually, I guess it kind of is good you ran out. It means you had a full house. Right?"

Words were just streaming out of my mouth now with absolutely no regard to if they made sense or were necessary. It was like I was trying to keep her engaged and was willing to continue to do so in the face of her clearly being repulsed by the sound of my voice. My jaw opened to continue yapping, but thankfully I couldn't think of anything else to say, and it slowly, sadly shut.

"Milk, eggs, whipping cream. Anything else?" she asked, her back now turned to me as she examined a frozen door with a few microwavable meals in it. I was really hoping she wasn't about to put a dozen or so in her hand cart and call that dinner tonight.

"Sugar. You were looking a little low earlier today."

"Sugar," she said, interrupting me and putting the packet in the cart. She had made her way past the freezer without putting anything in it, thankfully.

"Nutmeg, salt, and cinnamon I remember seeing in the spice cabinet," I said. "You'll need vanilla extract, though."

Nodding, she walked further down the aisle with the baking goods and found the spices. A few moments later, she raised a small bottle of the extract up and looked at me. I nodded, and she dropped it into the basket.

"Anything else?" she asked.

"That's it," I said. "Except, of course, the rum."

"Oh, god."

Ten minutes and a nice, long conversation about the legal and colloquial differences between what the differences between bourbon, whisky, whiskey, and scotch were and we had a bottle of Kentucky's finest in our bag to go along with the required bottle of rum with us and were on the road back to the bed-and-breakfast.

While I had been interested in what the old man had to say, being curious and not entirely sure the differences myself, Holly had glassed over and went silent. However, by the time we paid and left, she seemed to be a little bit cheerier. Maybe it was the dark chocolate bar she'd bought with the sea salt and caramel. Whatever the reason, it wasn't Christmas music. The second we left, a car passed blaring Mariah Carey's contribution to the Christmas Zeitgeist, and Holly got a look that I was fairly certain was her trying to utilize the Force to lift the car and send it careening into space.

I opted to keep the volume low on the eighties station on the way back, but a healthy dose of new-wave bands got her smiling a little by the time we got to the building. I parked and helped her get the groceries inside and began staging a station for me to brew the eggnog. It was my surprise when Holly didn't simply leave the room and instead came back in, putting on an apron and tying her hair behind her head, standing close to me on one side.

"Okay, what's first?" she asked.

I decided not to mention the fact that I had been planning on doing this myself and instead stepped back a foot or so.

"Crack the eggs and sugar in a bowl and whisk them," I said. "I'll get the saucepan going with everything else."

Nodding, she went about the task of whisking by hand, which again I didn't interrupt. There was an electric mixer in the drawer right in front of her, but I got the impression the violent circular motions she was going through in that bowl represented the expelling of some kind of pent-up aggression. I had zero desire to stop that.

Stirring the mixture until it simmered, I took the bowl from Holly and added a big spoonful in, whisking vigorously. I repeated this, and on the third spoonful, Holly took over.

"Why are you putting this stuff in so slow?" she asked.

"Tempering it," I said. "All at once and it would make scrambled eggs."

"Ahh." She fell silent until the last batch of mixture was in the saucepan. "I think it's done."

"Taste it. See what you think."

"You first," she said.

"Nope," I said. "I don't matter. This is about you. Besides, I like it with the rum in."

"Fine." She took a tasting spoon out and filled it. She put it to her lips and sucked it down, making a face and tossing the spoon away. "That was awful," she said, matter-of-factly.

I laughed, hard. This was going to be hard. Not the eggnog. The fact that even with her being cold and distant, I still found my feelings for her getting stronger.

I couldn't give up just yet. At least not until the holidays were over and I had to go. Until then, I was going to focus on any kind of fun we could have.

For now, that meant pulling out the bottle of rum.

Chapter Forty-One

Holly

IT TOOK A BIT OF CONVINCING for Lawson to get me to accept the eggnog tasted like it was supposed to and that people would enjoy it. I just couldn't wrap my head around somebody willingly gulping down the thick, sweet drink. It occurred to me that Lawson said this stuff wasn't like what was bought in a store, and I couldn't even imagine what drinking that stuff would be like.

But everybody's tastes were different, I told myself as we poured the batches we created into a large crystal bowl and settled the ladle into it. These people wanted eggnog; I enjoyed mayonnaise sandwiches as a child. What made us different was what made us beautiful and all that.

Dipping into the hopeful pro-individuality mindset of eighties music made me feel a little better about bringing our creation out into the living room for the guests. This was something they'd specifically asked for, and I didn't want to disappoint them.

Lawson had set up a card table and covered it with a cloth to create a display for the eggnog. He brought in the large bowl of eggnog as I brought in the glasses. I added a plastic cup for Vint, not thinking it would be the best idea to hand a fragile crystal cup to a little boy excited about Christmas.

"Is everything ready for the singalong?" I asked Lawson.

"Yep," he said. "I have it all cued up." He looked around the room. "You know, having a piano in one of these rooms would be a really great addition. It would be awesome to have live music for things like this. That would be so much more traditional for a singalong."

"Well, that would mean I'd also need someone capable of playing live music on a piano, since I don't think spontaneously being able to play the piano would be a good use of one of my Christmas miracles."

Lawson chuckled. "I don't think those work like wishes. You don't get doled out a specific number of them at the beginning of the season and ask for them to happen."

I looked over at him and felt my heart squeeze. He was right.

"The music coming through the speakers will be fine," I said, then hurried back into the kitchen before he could see the emotion welling up inside me.

I didn't really have any reason to be in the kitchen. We'd already brought all the glasses and the eggnog out into the living room. But I needed something to look like there was a point to my departure, so I grabbed some crackers and sliced up a couple of blocks of cheese to make a snack for the guests. By the time I got back to the living room with the tray, Nancy was already there.

She was eyeing the eggnog critically like just looking at it would tell her what it tasted like and if we'd succeeded. I set the crackers and cheese down beside the bowl and mustered up the biggest smile I could.

"Good evening, Nancy," I said. "I'm so glad you decided to join us for the singalong tonight."

"I don't sing," she said firmly.

"Neither do I," I said.

"Then why are you having a singalong?"

I opened my mouth to say something, but nothing came out. Closing it, I turned and walked away from the table, going over to Lawson where he was setting up the music.

"Why are we having a singalong?" I asked.

He lifted an eyebrow at me. "I thought we talked about that. It's a Christmas tradition. People like to get together and sing Christmas songs." He flashed a slightly teasing smile. "Most people."

"You know who isn't in that most people? Nancy. She came to a singalong to not sing."

"It's going to be fine," Lawson said. "Everybody is going to enjoy it. I promise."

The music started coming out of his phone, and he tucked his hand behind my head to pull it closer so he could press a kiss to my forehead. Tears stung in my eyes, and I scolded myself for it. I pulled away from him.

"I just realized I didn't change. I'll be right back," I said.

I rushed to my room and closed the door behind me. A couple of deep breaths lessened the painful tightness in my throat and helped me get a hold of myself. I considered splashing some cold water on my face, but that would just mean ruining my makeup, and I didn't want to leave the guests alone for as long as it would take to scrub it all off and reconstruct it. Instead, I stripped off my clothes to replace them with black pants and a sweater.

It wasn't an ugly Christmas sweater, but it was burgundy, and that was going to have to be enough.

Back in the living room, Lawson was chatting with the other guests and steering them toward the eggnog. I heard them laughing and could only imagine he was performing a retelling of the story of us making it. He might have been exaggerating about it a little considering the way the guests were reacting. Whatever he was saying, they found it hilarious.

Lawson looked up and noticed me standing in the doorway. He grinned and gestured for me to come over.

"Alright, everybody," he said. "Holly's here, so let's get started on this singalong!"

With fewer than twenty guests staying at the bed-and-breakfast, there wasn't exactly a huge crowd to go wild at the announcement, but a few of them cheered. I noticed Nancy was sitting in one of the armchairs at the side of the room, her legs crossed primly and a cup of eggnog in her hand. She didn't look thrilled at the singalong announcement, but she lifted the cup to her lips regularly. At least it seemed I was getting her stamp of approval on that.

Lawson went over to the phone and cued up the instrumental music for the first song on our list. As the guests took their cups and gathered closer around the tree, I wondered if we should have thought about printing out lyrics. But pretty quickly my worries about some of the guests not knowing the words to the songs disappeared as they burst out singing.

He looked at me and gave a bob of his head, trying to get me to come closer. I stayed where I was, wanting to just kind of observe and warm up before throwing myself into the seasonal jubilation. The guests sang and laughed, drinking the eggnog and occasionally toasting each other. I tried to enjoy it, getting myself a napkin full of cheese and crackers and inching closer to start humming along, but my heart felt so heavy it was hard to get whipped up into the spirit.

The music transitioned from a traditional carol to one of the fun, bouncy children's songs, and Lawson started dancing. His silliness was genuine rather than it looking like he was showing off, and I noticed even Nancy was starting to tap her toe and bob her head along with the song. It brought a smile to my lips, and I had a brief moment of happiness, but it didn't take long for everything to come back. As soon as I remembered that happiness went away, and everything just felt harder.

In between songs, I noticed a couple of the adult guests go over to the mantle and pick up the bottle of rum Lawson got when we were shopping for eggnog ingredients. They tipped a healthy amount into the nearly empty eggnog glasses, then went over to the bowl to top them off with more eggnog. Taking sips brought out nods and little sounds of approval.

Ian, Nancy's son who was traveling with her, went for the bottle and brought it over to his mother. She lifted the glass eagerly, and he poured some in. She smiled and nodded when she took a sip.

"Now it's perfect," she said.

Booze to the rescue.

Curious, I went over to the table and got a glass, put half a ladle of eggnog into it, and then made my way to the mantle, where Ian had replaced the bottle. I added some of the rum to the drink, thought about it for a second, and added more. It gave the eggnog a darker color, and I stared at it, wondering if this was a bad idea.

What the hell. I already hated eggnog. Adding rum to it could not possibly make it any worse.

I took a cautious sip. It didn't immediately taste horrible. I tried a slightly larger sip. It actually wasn't bad. Apparently, that was the secret. Spike your eggnog, and it became palatable.

I finished the glass and made myself another one. Another bottle of rum along with some whiskey and bourbon I had in the cabinets arrived on the mantle, and pretty soon, I was joining in on the singing. I couldn't absolutely promise I was in tune or even that I was singing the same song as everyone else, but I was in their midst and giving it my all.

A couple of times Lawson looked over at me with a raised eyebrow, but I ignored him. He wanted me to be festive, so there I was. Jingling my bells and counting down the twelve days.

When the bowl was almost empty and Vint was already curled up asleep on the couch, the guests called it a night and drifted out of the living room toward the stairs. I was still in the middle of the living room, swaying to the softer music coming out of Lawson's phone and nursing another eggnog. This one had whiskey in it. Maybe. It had something in it.

"Did you have fun?" Lawson asked.

I lifted the glass toward him in a toast. "Merry almost Christmas."

"Alright," he said with a laugh. "I'll help you clean up, and then you should get to bed."

"Maybe I don't want to," I said, taking another sip.

"What is going on with you?"

"Did you know eggnog is so much better with rum? Like... so much better," I said.

He nodded. "That's why people drink it that way."

"Did you have any?"

"No."

I went over to the table and made him a glass. I dumped the rest of the bottle of rum into it and pressed it into his hand. He sipped it and gave the nod I was starting to think was some sort of international symbol for something tasting better when spiked.

We started cleaning up, though in retrospect, I probably wasn't the most helpful person. I was too busy thinking about everything that happened and wondering why my Christmas had to turn out like this. Before I could stop myself, it all came tumbling out.

"So, when were you going to tell me you had some girl waiting for you when you go home? Monica. What kind of name is that? And why didn't you just say something? Why couldn't you be like... 'Hey, Holly, I'm pretending real life doesn't exist while I'm here, so I'm going to fool around with you, but then when this whole sparkling Christmas nonsense is over, I'm going home with my house and my girlfriend and my regular clothes and my bathing suits because it won't be winter eventually.'"

Lawson paused in the doorway of the living room, holding the eggnog bowl. He blinked at me a couple of times, and I tossed back the last of my drink.

Chapter Forty-Two

Lawson

"WHAT THE HELL ARE YOU talking about?" I asked.

Holly froze, her facial expression a mask of confusion and anger. Tears welled up in the corners of her eyes, and she cocked her head sideways, like she couldn't believe I would ask that.

The eggnog must have been especially strong. Whatever ratio Nancy demanded for her alcohol to eggnog must have been enough to put down an entire battalion, because Holly only had a couple of them, and I couldn't make heads or tails of what she was talking about.

"I heard you," she said, her words slurring as she pointed with one finger and held herself upright on the arm of the couch with the other hand. Her most recent eggnog sloshed in the pointing hand, but she didn't seem to notice. "I heard what you said when you thought I wasn't listening. I heard you on the phone. You were so excited to get back to her. I just want to know why?"

"Why what?" I asked, still confused. She overheard me on the phone? I didn't even remember talking on the phone in front of her. And what could I have possibly said that would have upset her so badly?

"Why did you even tell me about having a crush on me? Huh? Was this some... some... some twisted way of fulfilling your teenage fantasy? Is that it?" she said. Her voice wasn't loud, but it was loud enough. Even

41

though everyone else had long gone to bed, it wouldn't be strange if someone overheard them. Voices carry.

"Wait," I said, things clicking together finally and realization dawning on me. "Are you talking about when I was on the phone at the festival?"

"Yes," she said, her voice low and gravelly. "I heard you talk about your Monica."

It was like she spat the words out, especially the name. I sighed.

"Actually," I said, shifting my weight as I leaned against the doorframe, "you couldn't be further from the truth. Monica is one of my business partners. She invested quite a bit of money in very early and as such owns a percentage of the profits we make every year."

"What profits? What do you mean 'we' make?" she asked.

There was no use now. The cat was out of the bag. I had to tell her the truth, all of it, and in as much detail as she needed in order to get it all out.

"The company I work for... I own it," I said. "Monica was a childhood friend of mine, and she invested a large amount of cash—cash she got from her wealthy father—to help me start a business. Through busting my ass and spending more waking hours than I should have, I have built it into somewhat of an empire. When I told my assistant to tell Monica to pick somewhere to eat in celebration, it was because we just secured an acquisition that will take us from the biggest company in our industry in the Midwest to one of the largest companies in the country."

"So..." she began, the words processing in her mind so individually that I could almost see them sink in and her eyes widen, then darken again. "You and Monica aren't together?"

Despite myself, I laughed, walking back into the room and sitting on the couch next to her.

"It's not funny," Holly said, her bottom lip sticking out a little like she was pouting. It was a completely involuntary facial tic, and one I was sure she was aware of and put a stop to when she was sober. But she clearly was holding on to sobriety with a fingertip at this point.

"Monica and I have been friends since we were twelve," I said. "I was the first person she came out to."

"Came... out... to?"

"She's gay, Holly," I said. "Has a wife. They live happily, and very wealthily, together with their two kids, a dog, and a mansion that could fit all of Snowflake Hollow in the acreage of."

"Oh," she said, her voice falling faint. She sat back onto the armrest a bit as she turned completely toward me, pulling her legs up and crossing them in front of her.

"Yeah. So, I'm not exactly her type."

"But you never said anything about owning a company," she said. "Why would you lie to me?"

"I'm sorry about that." I could have argued the semantics of what a lie was and how I didn't necessarily lie to her outright, but a lie of omission was still a lie. I intentionally misled her into believing I was just some normal schmuck. Not a multimillionaire, and soon, most likely a billionaire.

"Sorry? You're some bigwig, and you pretended to be... normal. Like me."

"I am normal," I said. "I grew up just like you. I lived just like you until I was out of college. Monica never flashed her money around, and her dad was the one with all of it. He lived in another state, and all I knew was she went to visit him, and *he* was wealthy. I didn't put it together that meant she was wealthy too. She lived just like I did. When she offered to invest in my company, it wasn't some huge amount either. It was everything I needed to get going, but it wasn't more than I could have gotten from a bank if I had perfect credit and been in business for ten years already. She just moved me ahead a few steps."

"But you are rich now," she said, almost like a question. I hung my head.

"Yes."

"So, I'm just some girl you're having fun with while you're on vacation," she said. "Rich guys like you, ones who hide who they are and stay at a bed-and-breakfast in Snowflake Hollow..."

I didn't even want her to finish that thought.

"No. This is more. So much more. Everything I said about you before, it's true. One hundred percent. I have feelings for you, and they are stronger than I have ever felt." I scooted closer to her and picked up her hands, pulling them toward me. She didn't resist. "Holly, I'm falling for you. None of this changes how I feel."

"Really?" she asked, her eyes swimming with tears. I could almost see the tension and relief flood from her as her shoulders sagged and her body leaned closer.

"Really," I said.

"Oh, Lawson." She threw her arms around me and stood on her knees on the couch.

Quickly, she lost her balance, and we tumbled, me going backward and pulling her on top of me to protect her. As soon as my head hit the couch cushion, her lips crushed into mine, and I sank into the kiss.

Holly ran her hands down my side and shuffled her body so she was straddling me. I could feel the heat coming off her body, her chest rising and falling rapidly and her breasts brushing my stomach. I wanted her. I wanted her bad, and my cock pressed against the zipper of my pants, dying for me to unleash him.

But the smell of the rum was strong on her breath. She was drunk. It wasn't right.

"Hang on," I said, pulling her up and stopping her. "Not right now. You've had too much to drink."

"No..." she began, but I shook my head.

"Not until you're sober," I said. "Come on. Let's go outside and look at the decorations."

"It's cold out there."

"Good," I responded, sitting up. "You might sober up faster. As it is, you are going to have a hell of a headache in the morning."

"Fine." She rolled her eyes, but for once, it didn't have the venom or dismissal that it had the last couple of days. "But I am bringing this."

She held up her eggnog, and I swiped it from her easily.

"Hey," she began.

"This is mine now," I said. "You drink water. You're going to need it." I walked over to the coatrack and grabbed her coat and scarf. "Here, put this on."

"Okay," she said, stomping over in mock childishness.

I helped her get her coat on, which wasn't without its adventures, and got a large, bottled water out of the refrigerator for her. We went outside, and she stumbled as she walked, but I kept her upright. We admired the decorations for a little while before I noticed she was starting to sober up a bit. I, on the other hand, was headed the other way, having brought a much larger glass of eggnog with me. It was mostly rum.

"I'm really tired," she said after a little while, her head resting on my shoulder as we watched the twinkling lights.

"I bet. Come on. Let's get you to bed," I said.

I could feel the tension between us as we made our way up the stairs, the unspoken question of if I would join her in the room. She was sobering up, and I had probably had enough rum to knock out a moose, but I was still pretty levelheaded about her. I didn't want to do anything that could put me back in the dark place we had been in the last few days. That included anything that could be felt like taking advantage of her.

Instead, as we reached her door, I pulled her in for a kiss and then turned on my heel. I could hear her behind me moan sadly, but I held up my hand above my head for a tiny wave.

"Good night, Holly. Finish your water before you go to sleep," I said.

"Good night," she said.

Before I reached my own door, I heard hers clicking shut behind me and smiled.

THE END
OF
PART 7

Snowflake
HOLLOW
12 DAYS OF CHRISTMAS
ADVENT CALENDARS
3
12
7
5
10
9
2
4
6
1
8
11
NEW CHAPTER EVERY DAY

Find Lexy Timms:

LEXY TIMMS NEWSLETTER:
http://www.lexytimms/newsletter
Lexy Timms Facebook Page:
https://www.facebook.com/SavingForever
Lexy Timms Website:
http://www.lexytimms.com

Lexy Timms
BOSS Book 3
BOSS Book 2
BOSS Book 1
Managing BOSSES Books 1-3
Lexy Timms
FREE
for a
Limited
Time

Want

FREE READS?

Sign up for Lexy Timms' newsletter
And she'll send you updates on new releases,
ARC copies of books and a whole lotta fun!

Sign up for news and updates!
http://www.lexytimms/newsletter

Holiday Romance by Lexy Timms

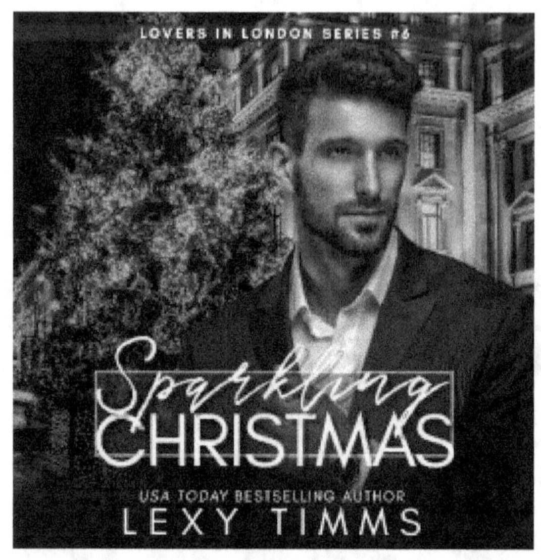

LOVERS IN LONDON SERIES #6
Sparkling
CHRISTMAS
USA TODAY BESTSELLING AUTHOR
LEXY TIMMS

Billionaire Holiday Romance Series Book One
DRIVING HOME FOR
Christmas
USA TODAY BESTSELLING AUTHOR
LEXY TIMMS
LIMITED TIME
Lexy Timms
FREE
DOWNLOAD

Fake
BILLIONAIRE
SERIES
Fake
CHRISTMAS
USA TODAY BESTSELLING AUTHOR
LEXY TIMMS

All
Wrapped
Up
LEXY TIMMS

Don't miss out!

Visit the website below and you can sign up to receive emails whenever Lexy Timms publishes a new book. There's no charge and no obligation.

https://books2read.com/r/B-A-NNL-JGUTB

BOOKS 2 READ

Connecting independent readers to independent writers.

Did you love *Snowflake Hollow - Part 7*? Then you should read *The Night Before Christmas*[1] by Lexy Timms!

Christmas isn't a season, it's a feeling.

It's Christmas and the family is together. Alex spent all of December home and their relationship has never been better.

But he's going back to work soon, and it's casting a dark cloud over everything for Jamie. It's silly but suddenly she's terrified of being alone again.

What if something goes wrong? What if she can't do it all alone? What if it turns out the kids like Alex better than they like her? There are so many things she needs to think about and work through, and its taking away from her time with the family.

---

1. https://books2read.com/u/mYp2JP

2. https://books2read.com/u/mYp2JP

When Jamie finally has the courage to talk to Alex, it comes out all wrong and only drives a wedge between them that threatens to ruin the last few days they have together at home.

Jamie needs to learn to trust herself, trust Alex, and not give into her doubts. Can she learn that before it's too late?

Managing the Bosses Series: The Boss The Boss Too Who's the Boss Now * Gift for the Boss (Christmas Novella) Love the Boss I Do the Boss Wife to the Boss Employed by the Boss Brother to the Boss Senior Advisor to the Boss Forever the Boss

Christmas with the Boss

Billionaire in Control

Billionaire Makes Millions

Billionaire at Work

Mark's Story - Precious Little Thing

Mark's Story - Priceless Love

NOVELLA Series: Valentine Love

The Cost of Freedom

Trick or Treat

The Night Before Christmas

Read more at www.lexytimms.com.

Also by Lexy Timms

12 Days of Christmas
Snowflake Hollow - Part 1
Snowflake Hollow - Part 2
Snowflake Hollow - Part 3
Snowflake Hollow - Part 4
Snowflake Hollow - Part 5
Snowflake Hollow - Part 6
Snowflake Hollow - Part 7

A Bad Boy Bullied Romance
I Hate You
I Hate You A Little Bit
I Hate You A Little Bit More

A Bump in the Road Series
Expecting Love
Selfless Act
Doctor's Orders

A Burning Love Series
Spark of Passion
Flame of Desire
Blaze of Ecstasy

A Chance at Forever Series
Forever Perfect
Forever Desired
Forever Together

A Dark Mafia Romance Series
Taken By The Mob Boss
Truce With The Mob Boss
Taking Over the Mob Boss
Trouble For The Mob Boss
Tailored By The Mob Boss
Tricking the Mob Boss

A Dating App Series
I've Been Matched
You've Been Matched
We've Been Matched

A "Kind of" Billionaire

Taking a Risk
Safety in Numbers
Pretend You're Mine

A Maybe Series
Maybe I Should
Maybe I Shouldn't
Maybe I Did

Assisting the Boss Series
Billion Reasons
Duke of Delegation
Late Night Meetings
Delegating Love
Suitors and Admirers

BBW Romance Series
Capturing Her Beauty
Pursuing Her Dreams
Tracing Her Curves

Beating the Biker Series
Making Her His
Making the Break
Making of Them

Betrayal at the Bay Series
Devil's Bay
Devil's Deceit
Devil's Duplicity

Billionaire Banker Series
Banking on Him
Price of Passion
Investing in Love
Knowing Your Worth
Treasured Forever
Banking on Christmas
Billionaire Banker Box Set Books #1-3

Billionaire CEO Brothers
Tempting the Player
Late Night Boardroom
Reviewing the Perfomance
Result of Passion
Directing the Next Move
Touching the Assets

Billionaire Hitman Series
The Hit
The Job
The Run

Billionaire Holiday Romance Series
Driving Home for Christmas
The Valentine Getaway
Cruising Love
Billionaire Holiday Romance Box Set

Billionaire in Disguise Series
Facade
Illusion
Charade

Billionaire Secrets Series
The Secret
Freedom
Courage
Trust
Impulse
Billionaire Secrets Box Set Books #1-3

Blind Sight Series
See Me
Fix Me
Eyes On Me

Branded Series
Money or Nothing
What People Say
Give and Take

Building Billions
Building Billions - Part 1
Building Billions - Part 2
Building Billions - Part 3

Butler & Heiress Series
To Serve
For Duty
No Chore
All Wrapped Up

Change of Heart Series
The Heart Needs
The Heart Wants
The Heart Knows

Counting the Billions
Counting the Days
Counting On You

Counting the Kisses

Cry Wolf Reverse Harem Series
Beautiful & Wild
Misunderstood
Never Tamed

Darkest Night Series
Savage
Vicious
Brutal
Sinful
Fierce

Diamond in the Rough Anthology
Billionaire Rock
Billionaire Rock - part 2

Dirty Little Taboo Series
Flirting Touch
Denying Pleasure
Forbidding Desire
Craving Passion

Dominating PA Series

Her Personal Assistant - Part 1
Her Personal Assistant - Part 2
Her Personal Assistant Box Set

Fake Billionaire Series
Faking It
Temporary CEO
Caught in the Act
Never Tell A Lie
Fake Christmas
Fake Billionaire Box Set #1-3

Firehouse Romance Series
Caught in Flames
Burning With Desire
Craving the Heat
Firehouse Romance Complete Collection

Forging Billions Series
Dirty Money
Petty Cash
Payment Required

For His Pleasure
Elizabeth
Georgia

Madison

Fortune Riders MC Series
Billionaire Biker
Billionaire Ransom
Billionaire Misery
Fortune Riders Box Set - Books #1-3

Fragile Series
Fragile Touch
Fragile Kiss
Fragile Love

Great Temptation Series
The Devil's Footsteps
Heaven's Command
Mortals Surrender

Hades' Spawn Motorcycle Club
One You Can't Forget
One That Got Away
One That Came Back
One You Never Leave
One Christmas Night
Hades' Spawn MC Complete Series

Hard Rocked Series
Rhyme
Harmony
Lyrics

Heart of Stone Series
The Protector
The Guardian
The Warrior

Heart of the Battle Series
Celtic Viking
Celtic Rune
Celtic Mann
Heart of the Battle Series Box Set

Heistdom Series
Master Thief
Goldmine
Diamond Heist
Smile For Me
Your Move
Green With Envy
Saving Money

Highlander Wolf Series
Pack Run
Pack Land
Pack Rules

Hollyweird Fae Series
Inception of Gold
Disruption of Magic
Guardians of Twilight

How To Love A Spy
The Secret
The Secret Life
The Secret Wife

Just About Series
About Love
About Truth
About Forever
Just About Box Set Books #1-3

Justice Series
Seeking Justice
Finding Justice

Chasing Justice
Pursuing Justice
Justice - Complete Series

Karma Series
Walk Away
Make Him Pay
Perfect Revenge

Kissed by Billions
Kissed by Passion
Kissed by Desire
Kissed by Love

Leaning Towards Trouble
Trouble
Discord
Tenacity

Love on the Sea Series
Ships Ahoy
Rough Sea
High Tide

Lovers in London Series

Risking Millions
Venture Capital
Worth the Expense
The Price of Luxury
Exclusive Passion

Love You Series
Love Life
Need Love
My Love

Managing the Billionaire
Never Enough
Worth the Cost
Secret Admirers
Chasing Affection
Pressing Romance
Timeless Memories
Managing the Billionaire Box Set Books #1-3

Managing the Bosses Series
The Boss
The Boss Too
Who's the Boss Now
Love the Boss
I Do the Boss
Wife to the Boss
Employed by the Boss

Brother to the Boss
Senior Advisor to the Boss
Forever the Boss
Christmas With the Boss
Billionaire in Control
Billionaire Makes Millions
Billionaire at Work
Precious Little Thing
Priceless Love
Valentine Love
The Cost of Freedom
Trick or Treat
The Night Before Christmas
Gift for the Boss - Novella 3.5
Managing the Bosses Box Set #1-3
Managing the Bosses Novellas

Mislead by the Bad Boy Series
Deceived
Provoked
Betrayed

Model Mayhem Series
Shameless
Modesty
Imperfection

Moment in Time

Highlander's Bride
Victorian Bride
Modern Day Bride
A Royal Bride
Forever the Bride

Mountain Millionaire Series
Close to the Ridge
Crossing the Bluff
Climbing the Mount

My Best Friend's Sister
Hometown Calling
A Perfect Moment
Thrown in Together

My Darker Side Series
Darkest Hour
Time to Stop
Against the Light

Neverending Dream Series
Neverending Dream - Part 1
Neverending Dream - Part 2
Neverending Dream - Part 3
Neverending Dream - Part 4

Neverending Dream - Part 5
Neverending Dream Box Set Books #1-3

Outside the Octagon
Submit
Fight
Knockout

Protecting Diana Series
Her Bodyguard
Her Defender
Her Champion
Her Protector
Her Forever
Protecting Diana Box Set Books #1-3

Protecting Layla Series
His Mission
His Objective
His Devotion

Racing Hearts Series
Rush
Pace
Fast

Regency Romance Series
The Duchess Scandal - Part 1
The Duchess Scandal - Part 2

Reverse Harem Series
Primals
Archaic
Unitary

Roommate Wanted Series
The Roommate

R&S Rich and Single Series
Alex Reid
Parker
Sebastian

Saving Forever
Saving Forever - Part 1
Saving Forever - Part 2
Saving Forever - Part 3
Saving Forever - Part 4
Saving Forever - Part 5
Saving Forever - Part 6

Saving Forever Part 7
Saving Forever - Part 8
Saving Forever Boxset Books #1-3

Secrets & Lies Series
Strange Secrets
Evading Secrets
Inspiring Secrets
Lies and Secrets
Mastering Secrets
Alluring Secrets
Secrets & Lies Box Set Books #1-3

Shifting Desires Series
Jungle Heat
Jungle Fever
Jungle Blaze

Sin Series
Payment for Sin
Atonement Within
Declaration of Love

Southern Romance Series
Little Love Affair
Siege of the Heart

Freedom Forever
Soldier's Fortune

Spanked Series
Passion
Playmate
Pleasure

Spelling Love Series
The Author
The Book Boyfriend
The Words of Love

Strength & Style
Suits You, Sir
Tailor Made
Perfect Gentleman

Taboo Wedding Series
He Loves Me Not
With This Ring
Happily Ever After

Tattooist Series
Confession of a Tattooist

Surrender of a Tattooist
Heart of a Tattooist
Hopes & Dreams of a Tattooist

Tennessee Romance
Whisky Lullaby
Whisky Melody
Whisky Harmony

The Bad Boy Alpha Club
Battle Lines - Part 1
Battle Lines

The Brush Of Love Series
Every Night
Every Day
Every Time
Every Way
Every Touch
The Brush of Love Series Box Set Books #1-3

The City of Mayhem Series
True Mayhem
Relentless Chaos
Broken Disorder

The Debt
The Debt: Part 1 - Damn Horse
The Debt: Complete Collection

The Fire Inside Series
Dare Me
Defy Me
Burn Me

The Gentleman's Club Series
Gambler
Player
Wager

The Golden Game
On The Pitch
Respect the Game
All Game
Sweat and Tears
The Final Score

The Golden Mail
Hot Off the Press
Extra! Extra!

Read All About It
Stop the Press
Breaking News
This Just In
The Golden Mail Box Set Books #1-3

The Lucky Billionaire Series
Lucky Break
Streak of Luck
Lucky in Love

The Millionaire's Pretty Woman Series
Perfect Stranger
Captive Devotion
Sweet Temptations

The Sound of Breaking Hearts Series
Disruption
Destroy
Devoted

The University of Gatica Series
The Recruiting Trip
Faster
Higher
Stronger

Dominate
No Rush
University of Gatica - The Complete Series

T.N.T. Series
Troubled Nate Thomas - Part 1
Troubled Nate Thomas - Part 2
Troubled Nate Thomas - Part 3

Toxic Touch Series
Noxious
Lethal
Willful
Tainted
Craved
Toxic Touch Box Set Books #1-3

Undercover Boss Series
Marketing
Finance
Legal

Undercover Series
Perfect For Me
Perfect For You
Perfect For Us

Unknown Identity Series
Unknown
Unpublished
Unexposed
Unsure
Unwritten
Unknown Identity Box Set: Books #1-3

Unlucky Series
Unlucky in Love
UnWanted
UnLoved Forever

War Torn Letters Series
My Sweetheart
My Darling
My Beloved

Wet & Wild Series
Stormy Love
Savage Love
Secure Love

Worth It Series

Worth Billions
Worth Every Cent
Worth More Than Money

You & Me - A Bad Boy Romance
Just Me
Touch Me
Kiss Me

Standalone
Wash
Loving Charity
Summer Lovin'
Love & College
Billionaire Heart
First Love
Frisky and Fun Romance Box Collection
Beating Hades' Bikers
Everyone Loves a Bad Boy
Dead of Night

Watch for more at www.lexytimms.com.

About the Author

"Love should be something that lasts forever, not is lost forever." Visit USA TODAY BESTSELLING AUTHOR, LEXY TIMMS https://www.facebook.com/SavingForever *Please feel free to connect with me and share your comments. I love connecting with my readers.* Sign up for news and updates and freebies - I like spoiling my readers! http://eepurl.com/9i0vD website: www.lexytimms.com Dealing in Antique Jewelry and hanging out with her awesome hubby and three kids, Lexy Timms loves writing in her free time. MANAGING THE BOSS-ES is a bestselling 10-part series dipping into the lives of Alex Reid and Jamie Connors. Can a secretary really fall for her billionaire boss?

Read more at www.lexytimms.com.